Tanna's Owl

by Rachel and Sean Qitsualik-Tinsley

illustrated by Yong Ling Kang

Published by Inhabit Media Inc.
www.inhabitmedia.com

Inhabit Media Inc. (Iqaluit) P.O. Box 11125, Iqaluit, Nunavut, X0A 1H0
(Toronto) 191 Eglinton Avenue East, Suite 310, Toronto, Ontario, M4P 1K1

Editors: Neil Christopher and Kelly Ward
Art director: Danny Christopher

This project was made possible in part by the Government of Canada.

We acknowledge the support of the Canada Council for the Arts for our publishing program.

Canada ▌◆▐   ❀ Canada Council   Conseil des Arts
              for the Arts   du Canada

Printed in Canada

Library and Archives Canada Cataloguing in Publication

Title: Tanna's owl / by Rachel and Sean Qitsualik-Tinsley ; illustrated by Yong Ling Kang.

Names: Qitsualik-Tinsley, Rachel, 1953- author. I Qitsualik-Tinsley, Sean, 1969- author. I Kang,
    Yong Ling, illustrator.

Identifiers: Canadiana 20190203617 I ISBN 9781772272505 (hardcover)

Classification: LCC PS8633.I88 T36 2020 I DDC jC813/.6–dc23

A Greeting from Rachel

I had a lot of strange pets growing up. That was how things were, way back. In the Arctic of many decades ago. Animals were around us all the time. We didn't just need them to survive. They were our companions. We used to respect them. Our ancient stories even said they were family!

Inuit have lots of names. That's because some of them are magical. Tanna is one of my magical names. It means "That One Over There." Owls are magical, too. Inuit were always careful, way back, to note whatever belonged to the Land, Sea, or Sky. And the most magical animals were those who brought these things together.

Owls, you see, can fly. But they're raised on the Land. So they bring Land and Sky together.

I'm about to tell you a little bit about my owl. In truth, it wasn't even "my" owl. I don't think you can really own an animal. Or a piece of Land. Or anything, actually. You can only bring things together. Learn to help. To care.

I wonder if my father wanted me to know that?

Summer began and Tanna's owl arrived.

Her father had returned from hunting. With him, he'd brought
an owl.

Why did Father get me such an ugly thing? thought Tanna.

The baby owl was round. Grey. Brown. Its eyes were big and yellow. Its beaky mouth seemed wide enough to swallow its own head.

But, Tanna thought, *it's somehow cute . . . .*

"You'll have to take good care of it," Father told her. "It has no mother. It'll need to eat two or three times a day."

That night Tanna set her alarm for four o'clock. A.M.! She had the shortest sleep of her life.

She had to catch lemmings. There was no bird food. And the owl wouldn't have eaten it, anyway. But her brothers and sisters helped.

Tanna named the owl Ukpik (the Inuktut for "owl").

Ukpik lived in her father's workshop. Tanna thought of the bird as a "she."

"Line the floor with papers," said Father, "as it will poop a lot."

When Ukpik did not get her food *right* away, *early* in the morning, she would stomp her feet.

She would sway back and forth.

She would chomp her beak.

At least she can communicate, Tanna thought to herself.

After feeding Ukpik, Tanna would stare into the bird's light golden eyes. She wondered if owls had thoughts.

"Father, does Ukpik know she's an owl?" asked Tanna.

"It knows you feed it," Father said, smiling.

Ukpik soon tired Tanna out. The owl became more and more demanding. No matter how much Tanna fed her, Ukpik still stomped. Swayed. Chomped.

Tanna wondered if the bird was sick. She took Ukpik outside and placed her on the ground.

"What do you want, you alien thing?" Tanna demanded.

Ukpik just stared at her. Then, creepily, the owl turned her head around backwards, watching the family dogs. Looking at Ukpik like that made Tanna's own neck feel sore.

Soon Tanna's brothers and sisters grew sick of catching lemmings.

"Owls need lemmings!" Tanna protested.

But they'd seen Ukpik eat. They said she was gross.

"Can Ukpik eat fish?" Tanna asked Father.

"It can probably eat whatever fits in its mouth," he told her.

Soon Ukpik was eating any kind of meat or fish. Even caribou!

The owl was no longer cute. Feeding her was an awful chore. Ukpik's beak was sharp as blades. She snatched at her food. Tanna had to wear gloves.

One rainy day, Tanna took Ukpik outside. The owl was no longer grey and brown. She was growing white plumes. The feathers on her feet were thick as polar bear fur. Her talons were like little black knives.

Ukpik looked around as though bored. Then she stared at the sky, as though to say,

I should be up there . . . .

Tanna picked up the owl and moved her up and down. Ukpik was too young to fly, but she started to flap her wings.

Maybe, thought Tanna, *pretending to fly will make her feel better.*

Summer ended. Tanna had to leave her community for school.

She worried about Ukpik, who had been left behind and had never flown.

But Tanna was happy not to get up at 4:00 a.m.

Or catch lemmings.

Or see stomping.

Or hear chomping.

When the next summer arrived, Tanna came home.

Ukpik was gone.

"It was grown," Father told her. "The owl didn't belong to us. It had to fly free."

She flew? thought Tanna. And she smiled.

25

One day, Tanna went walking. Even though Ukpik had been so much work, she missed the owl. A little.

Tanna picked an Arctic poppy—its golden petals like frozen sunlight.

Then she was startled by movement. Something white.

An *ukpik*!

The beautiful owl landed on a rocky hill, purpled with tiny flowers. It blinked at Tanna. Its eyes were the same colour as Tanna's poppy.

My Ukpik? Tanna wondered.

Bird and girl watched each other for a long time. Arctic winds stirred Tanna's black hair and the owl's white feathers.

Tanna didn't know if this was Ukpik. She wanted to believe, though. She wanted to think that Ukpik had come by—just to show how lovely she'd become.

Maybe, Tanna thought as she walked away, *beauty is worth some work.*

Rachel and Sean Qitsualik-Tinsley write fiction and educational works that celebrate the secretive world of Arctic cosmology and shamanism. Of Inuit-Cree ancestry, Rachel was born in a tent at the northernmost tip of Baffin Island. Raised as a boy, she learned Inuit survival lore from her father. Eventually, she survived residential school. Rachel specializes in archaic dialects and balances personal shamanic experience with a university education. She has published over four hundred articles on culture and language, been shortlisted for several awards, and has enjoyed many years as a judge for Historica Canada's Indigenous Arts & Stories competition. In 2012, she was awarded the Queen Elizabeth II Diamond Jubilee Medal for contributions to Canadian culture. Sean Qitsualik-Tinsley is of Scottish-Mohawk descent and learned a love of nature and stories from his father. He originally trained as an illustrator, but eventually discovered greater aptitude with words, his sci-fi work winning second place in the California-based Writers of the Future contest. Rachel and Sean sweepingly met at the Banff Centre, Alberta, spending subsequent decades as Arctic researchers and consultants. Together, they have published about a dozen books as English originals, along with many shorter works. They are inspired by the "imaginal intelligence" of pre-colonial, Arctic traditions (ancient Inuit and the now-extinct Tuniit). Many such works are found in K–12 schools and universities across Canada and abroad. Their young adult novel of historical fiction, Skraelings, won second prize in the Governor General's Literary Awards of 2014 and first prize for the Burt Award of 2015.

Yong Ling-Kang is an illustrator and avid comic book reader. She is inspired by simple, day-to-day experiences and her nostalgia for childhood. She suspects that her fondness for drawing may have been caused by watching too many cartoons. Yong Ling was raised in tropical Singapore, and as a result, she enjoys slow water sports and spicy food. She currently lives and works in Toronto where she enjoys reading comics and taking long walks in green spaces.

Notes on Inuktitut Pronunciation

There are some sounds in Inuktitut that may be unfamiliar to English speakers. The pronunciation below conveys those sounds in the following ways:

· A double vowel (e.g., aa, ee) lengthens the vowel sound.
· Capitalized letters denote the emphasis.

For additional Inuktitut-language resources, please visit inhabitmedia.com/inuitnipingit

Term	Pronunciation	Meaning
ukpik	OOK-pik	snowy owl